She asked her friends to help. "Will you help me dig the ground?"

"No," said the dog, "I'm too busy. Ask the cat."

"Will you help me sow the seeds?"
said the little red hen.

"No," said the cat, "I'm too busy.
Ask the mouse."

The
Little Red Hen

Gerald Rose

CAMBRIDGE
UNIVERSITY PRESS

One day, the little red hen found some wheat.
"I will plant this wheat so that I can have
flour to make some bread," she said.

So the little red hen dug the ground and
sowed the seeds all by herself.

When the seeds began to grow, the little red hen said, "Will you help me water the wheat?"

"No," said the mouse, "I'm too busy. Ask the horse."

So the little red hen watered the wheat
all by herself.
It grew tall.

"Will you help me cut the wheat?"
said the little red hen.

"No," said the horse, "I'm too busy.
Ask the sheep."

So the little red hen cut the wheat and
put the grain into a sack all by herself.

"Will you help me carry the grain?"
said the little red hen.

"No," said the sheep, "I'm too busy.
Ask the cow."

So the little red hen took the grain to the mill all by herself.

The miller ground the grain into flour. Then the little red hen took the flour home.

"Will you help me make the bread?"
said the little red hen.
"No," said the cow, "make it yourself."

So the little red hen baked the bread
all by herself.

"That bread smells good," said all her
friends. "Can we have some?"
"No," said the little red hen.

"You didn't help me
dig the ground,
sow the seeds,
water the wheat,
cut the wheat,
carry the grain or
bake the bread.

I have done the work all by myself,
so my chicks and I will eat the bread."